Harry and Kate at the Book Museum

Learning Resource Service

412596

SET
R
MCKE

For my nephew, Alex

Published in 2013 in Great Britain by
Barrington Stoke Ltd
18 Walker Street, Edinburgh, EH3 7LP

www.barringtonstoke.co.uk

This story was first published in a different form in
Wow! 366, Scholastic Children's Books, 2008

Text © 2008 Rosefire Ltd
Illustrations © Martin Remphry

The moral right of the author has been asserted
in accordance with the Copyright, Designs and
Patents Act 1988

Individual ISBN 978-1-78112-299-0
Pack ISBN 978-1-78112-308-9

Not available separately

Printed in China by Leo

www.barringtonstoke.co.uk

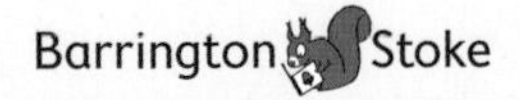

Sophie McKenzie

ILLUSTRATED BY MARTIN REMPHRY

Harry and Kate at the Book Museum

Mum, Harry and Kate were at the book museum.

“These books are very rare and worth a lot of money,” Mum said. “This is going to be great.”

Harry looked round. The museum was full of old glass cases. The books inside were dusty.

Harry was bored.

Even the security guard was snoring in the corner.

Then Harry saw a man hang his jacket over the CCTV camera on the wall.

The jacket covered the camera.

The man went over to a glass case. A very old, rare book was inside the case.

He took a metal lever from his pocket and forced open the case.

The security guard still snored in the corner.

Mum was looking at a book on the other side of the room.

"Look, Kate," Harry said.

Kate looked.

The man took the old, rare book out of the case.

He put it in his pocket and walked out a door that said 'Private'.

“Let’s follow him,” Kate said.

“And catch him,” said Harry.

They followed the thief out the door, down a corridor, round a corner, then along another corridor.

Soon they were going down the first corridor again.

The thief stopped.

Behind him, Harry and Kate stopped too.

They were standing near a sign that pointed to a door.

The sign said 'Storeroom this way'.

“I think he’s lost,” Kate whispered.

The thief turned.

He saw them.

Oh, no! Now he was walking up to them.

Harry's heart thumped. Where could they run?

"Oi, kids," the thief snapped. "Do you know the way out?"

Harry looked at the sign behind the thief.
He pointed to the storeroom.

"That's the way out," he said.

The thief walked into the storeroom.

Harry slammed the door shut.

Kate turned the key in the lock.

“We’ve got him!” said Harry.

“Hurray!” said Kate.

Harry and Kate went back to the museum. Mum was still looking at books. They told her how they'd trapped the thief.

Then Mum told the security guard.

The security guard rang the police, and the police arrested the thief.

“Well, that visit didn’t turn out like I expected,” Mum said, as they went home.

“But you were right about one thing,” Harry said with a grin. “It was great!”

Are you NUTS about stories?

Michael Morpurgo
All I Said Was ...
Illustrated by Ross Colli

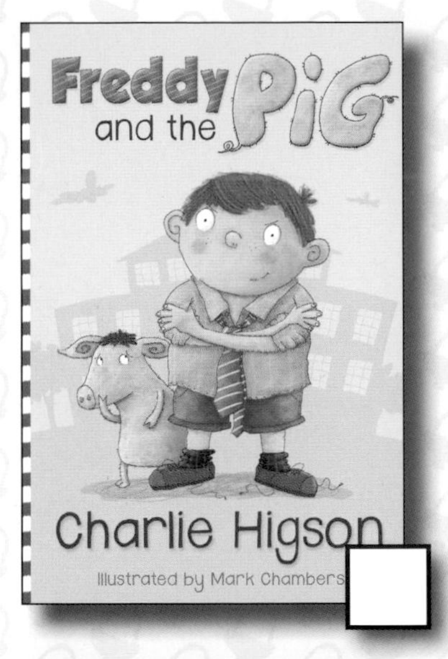
Freddy and the PiG
Charlie Higson
Illustrated by Mark Chambers

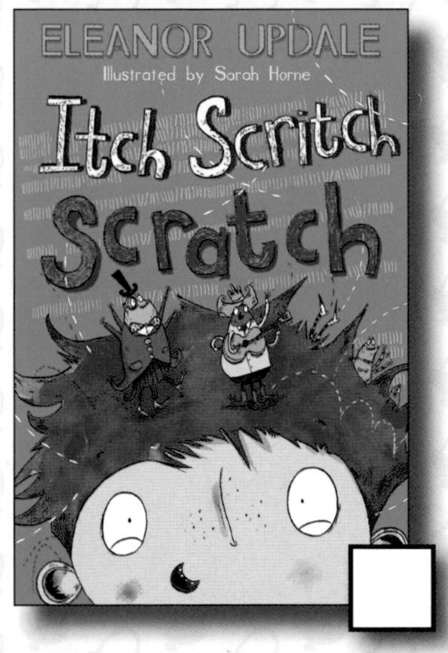
ELEANOR UPDALE
Illustrated by Sarah Horne
Itch Scritch Scratch

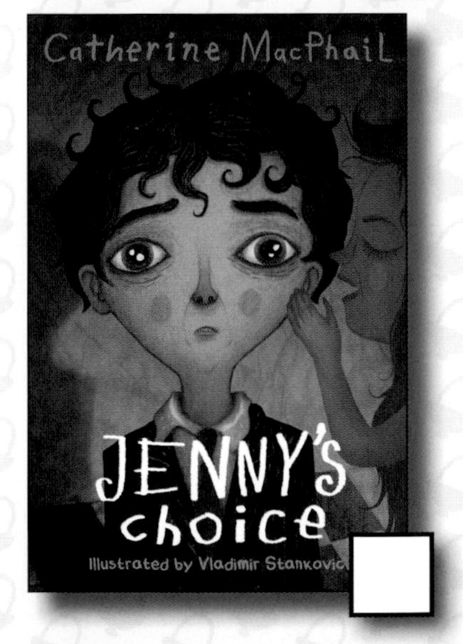
Catherine MacPhail
JENNY'S choice
Illustrated by Vladimir Stankovic

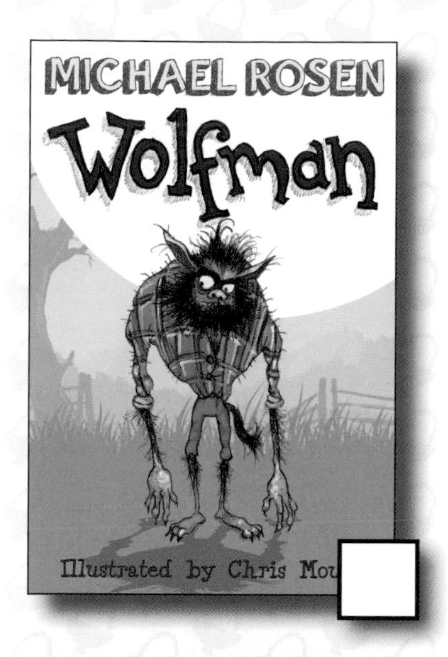

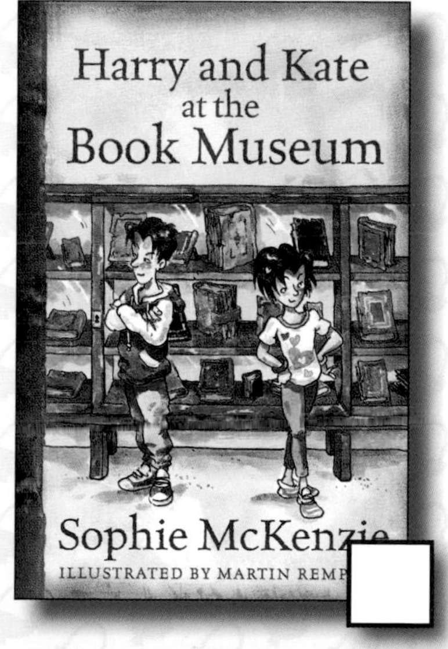

Read ALL the Acorns!

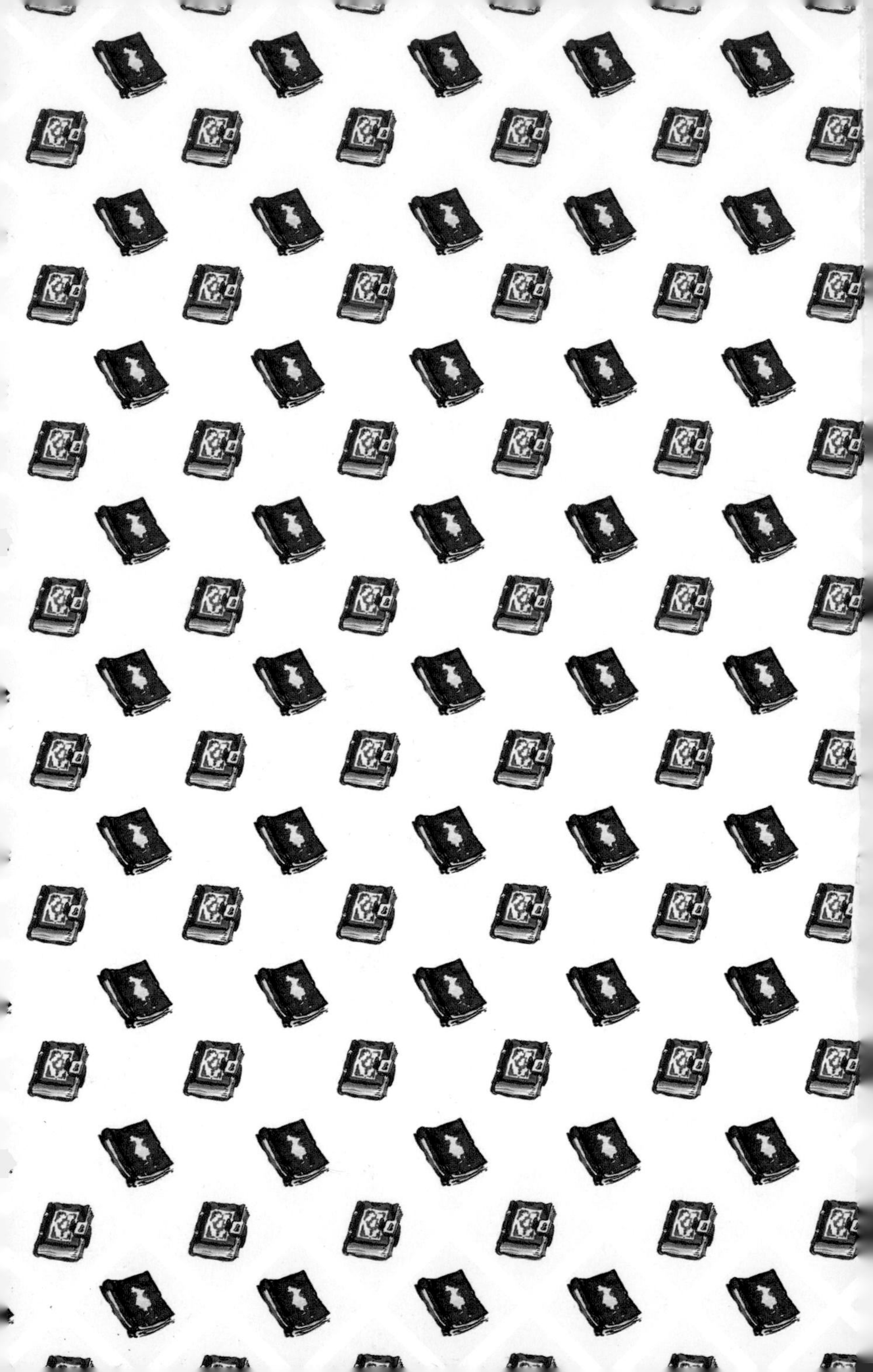